Beware
Princess!

Mary Hoffman

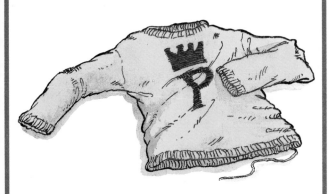

Illustrated by
CHRIS RIDDELL

HEINEMANN · LONDON

For Sarah, my dark princess

William Heinemann Ltd
Michelin House
81 Fulham Road
London
SW3 6RB

LONDON · MELBOURNE · AUCKLAND

First published 1986
Reprinted 1987, 1988
Text © Mary Hoffman 1986
Illustrations © Chris Riddell 1986

School packs of BANANA BOOKS are
available from Heinemann Educational Books

434 93038 5
Printed in Hong Kong by
Imago Publishing Ltd

Chapter One

POPPY WAS A princess, but she didn't
feel like one. Her parents were a King
and Queen and they lived in a castle
so she knew she must be a princess.
But Poppy had read a lot about
princesses, and she knew what they
were supposed to be like. They should
have long blonde hair, blue eyes and
pink cheeks. Poppy had short black
hair and brown eyes. She spent as
much time out of doors as she could,
so her face was nice and brown too.

Princesses in books always wore

beautiful dresses. Poppy was rather scruffy and though she *had* some beautiful dresses, they always seemed to end up torn and dirty. Beautiful dresses are no good if you like to play outdoors a lot.

The King and Queen were very traditional, the sort you'd never catch popping down to the shops without their crowns on. When they saw their daughter climbing trees or playing hopscotch with the castle guards, it sometimes made them wonder if Princess Poppy was really their own

flesh and blood – or a being from another world.

For the first nine years of her life, Poppy more or less had her own way. Although the King and Queen were perhaps a little disappointed by her, she was a great favourite with the castle guards, the cook and the gardener. Then on her ninth birthday, after a really royal tea – there were *some* advantages in being a princess – her parents took her aside for a serious talk.

'Now, my dear,' said the king, 'as you are the only heir to our throne, your mother and I thought it was time for you to start on some of your princessly duties.'

'Bother,' thought Poppy, 'I suppose I'll have to stop enjoying myself now. And I know I'll be no good at them.'

Out loud, she said, 'Yes, Father, but what *are* my princessly duties?'

The king began to look vague. 'Well,' he said.

'Don't beat about the bush, Algy,' interrupted the queen. 'Tell her about the ogre!'

Poppy opened her eyes wide. 'What ogre?'

'You see, my dear,' said the King, 'we have an ogre in the kingdom, of rather . . . er . . . *traditional* tastes.'

'Traditional be blowed,' said the Queen, rather rudely. 'The point is, Poppy, that like most ogres, his taste is for princesses.'

'To play with?' asked Poppy innocently.

'To eat,' said her mother.

Chapter Two

IT DIDN'T TAKE Poppy long to get used to the idea that an ogre was interested in having her for dinner. She had no intention of letting it happen, of course, but she didn't at all agree with her parents' plan for preventing it. Their idea was to lock her up in a tall, windowless tower, which they happened to have in the castle, with guards all around it, until a handsome knight came along and killed the ogre.

'But that might take ages,' objected Poppy. 'And I couldn't play outside. And who needs a knight anyway?'

'A princess who is on an ogre's menu,' said her mother, severely.

But Poppy eventually got the Queen and the King to agree to a slight change in the tower plan. And so, next morning, she was happily swinging on one of the top branches of a cherry-tree in the palace gardens, when she came face to face with an enormous belt-buckle. It was on a belt strapped round the bulging middle of the largest, ugliest creature she had ever seen. Poppy had to look up very high to see its face, and it wasn't really worth the effort. The ogre was peering short-sightedly towards the castle and puffing like a giant balloon-pump.

'Hullo, there,' shouted Poppy, in her loudest voice. But it was nothing

like as loud as the voice that replied.

'Hullo, yourself. What are you doing in that tree? Are you a bird or a boy?'

'Neither,' said Poppy, 'but never mind me. I bet I know what you're doing.'

'What?' boomed the ogre suspiciously, trying to get a clearer look at Poppy among the cherry leaves.

'Looking for the Princess,' she answered.

The ogre sighed and it made the ground tremble. 'That's right. Next on my list. The Princess Poppy.'

'Well, I can tell you where she is.'

'Go on then,' he whispered, nearly blowing Poppy off her branch.

'You see that tower, over by the west wall of the castle?'

'Yes.'

'With the guards all round it?'

'Yes.'

'In there.'

The ogre seemed to hesitate.

'What's she like?' he asked.

'Pink and plump.'

'Sounds delicious!' said the ogre,
but somehow he didn't sound as if he
meant it.

'What's the matter?' asked Poppy.

'Don't you fancy a nice tender little princess today?'

The ogre burped – a terrifying sound – then put his big, fat fingers up to his enormous mouth and blushed.

'Pardon,' he said. 'A touch of indigestion. I had rather too big a breakfast, of . . . '

Poppy did not want to know what he had had for breakfast so she interrupted quickly.

'If you don't mind my saying so, I don't think it would hurt you at all to go without lunch, in fact, it wouldn't hurt if you didn't eat for the next week.'

The ogre passed his huge hand over his bulging belly and looked puzzled.

'Wouldn't it? No princesses? No nothing?'

'That's right,' said Poppy firmly. 'A complete rest from food, followed by a complete change of diet. I don't think someone with a weight problem like yours ought to consider eating meat more than once a fortnight. And then not anything as rich as princess. Perhaps a lightly grilled chop or some chicken occasionally. But definitely not princess.'

The ogre groaned.

'I think you may be right. I've got a dreadful stomach-ache. But it is

traditional, you know, for ogres to eat boys and girls, particularly princesses.'

'What's the point of doing what's traditional if it gives you stomach-ache?' said Poppy.

The ogre had never thought of that. 'What shall I do then?'

'Eat these peppermints,' said Poppy, pulling a packet out of her jeans pocket and throwing it up to the ogre. 'And go and lie down somewhere until

you feel less full. Then every time
you start to feel peckish, remember
the tummy-ache and have a nice
omelette or something.'

The ogre looked at the peppermints

and popped the tiny packet, paper and all, into his huge mouth.

'Thank you,' he said, 'thank you, little bird – I'll give it a try.' As he stomped off, he turned back and waved. 'Tell them to let the princess out,' he bellowed, 'she's quite safe.'

Poppy slid down out of the tree and ran to tell the guards they could stop guarding the empty tower. Then she went to tell the King and Queen that the ogre was disposed of and to get some more peppermints.

Chapter Three

THE NEXT DAY, Poppy was enjoying some strawberries and cream when a terrific hullabaloo broke out at the castle gates. She was pretty sure it had nothing to do with the ogre. She had seen him in the distance, jogging, and nibbling at an uprooted tree as if it were a giant stick of celery. He looked a bit slimmer already.

Poppy wiped her mouth and looked over the battlements. Down by the portcullis was a very traditional knight. He wasn't exactly in shining armour. In fact, even at a distance his armour looked distinctly rusty. But it was all there. Plumed helmet, visor up, complete metal suit, sword, shield, lance and a particularly nasty-looking object with metal knobs on it hanging from his belt. No wonder he looked hot and bothered. His horse didn't look too happy either.

Just then the Queen came rushing out onto the battlements to find Poppy. She seemed very agitated.

'Oh, there you are. You'll never guess what's happened.'

'What?'

'The Cross Red Knight has arrived. And it's all your fault!' The Queen burst into tears.

'My fault?' asked Poppy, astonished. 'What have I got to do with it?'

'I sent for him. At least I sent for a knight. You know, because of the ogre,' said the Queen, dabbing at her eyes. 'And they've sent the wrong kind. This one doesn't rescue princesses at all. He just goes round issuing challenges to single combat and all that sort of thing.'

'Oh, mother,' said Poppy, rather touched. 'You really shouldn't have. I managed the ogre quite nicely by myself.'

'Well, yes, as it happens, you did,' admitted the Queen. 'But I wasn't to know that, was I? It's not at all traditional. And then I forgot to cancel the knight and he's fuming away at the gates, wanting to do battle with someone. I dare say he'd have made do with the ogre if we'd still had him.'

'There, there,' said Poppy, 'don't worry, I'll go and see what I can do. I think I'll just call in at the kitchen first, though.'

A few minutes later, Poppy persuaded a guard to let her slip through the portcullis. She was carrying a bucket of water and a covered basket. The Cross Red Knight was looking even crosser and redder than before. His visor was up and he was mopping his face with his handkerchief. It was a very hot day.

'Sire,' said Poppy, bowing low.

'Allow me to give your horse a drink
while you wait.'

The Cross Red Knight looked down
at Poppy. Cross as he was, he knew
what was due to a knight's horse.

'Very well,' he grumbled.

The knight dismounted with a great
clanking of rusty armour and his horse
thrust her nose eagerly into the bucket
of water.

'Warm day for jousting, Sire,' said
Poppy, politely.

'Harumph!' shouted the knight. 'I
don't see much chance of a joust here.
I've been standing at this gate for half

an hour and no one has accepted my challenge.'

'I don't suppose they would,' said Poppy. 'The king's too old and they have no son.'

The knight leaned against a stone wall, looking cross.

'Why don't you take off your helmet, Sire?' asked Poppy.

The knight hesitated, then removed his helmet. His face was very red and cross but he had quite nice fair hair which fluttered a bit in the breeze.

'Perhaps you would care for a little something yourself?' said Poppy, unpacking her basket.

The knight still looked very angry and uncomfortable but as Poppy spread out a checked tablecloth and laid it with a fresh green salad, cold white wine and a bowl of juicy cherries, he gradually began to sink to his knees. He couldn't bend or sit properly because of the armour so Poppy politely offered to help him off with it. The knight couldn't resist the cool, fresh lunch and was soon sitting eating it in his underwear. He began to look less red and cross.

'Why do you always want to fight people?' asked Poppy as she watched him arrange his cherry-stones neatly on the side of his plate.

'I don't want to,' said the knight, juicily, 'I have to. It's traditional. A knight like me has to go round

challenging other people to fight and the one who wins is the best knight.'

'There *are* other kinds of knight, I believe,' said Poppy, 'who rescue Princesses from ogres and have amazing adventures.'

The knight looked interested.

'I mean,' said Poppy, 'it doesn't

seem much of a job just beating people up all the time. And it must be awfully hot having to fight in all that armour. You could have a flowing green tunic if you were the other sort of knight and you could have a squire behind you on another horse with all your armour, in case you needed it.'

The knight looked very interested.

'That sounds much better,' he said. 'But I am supposed to be the Cross Red Knight. No one would think of sending for me to rescue anybody.'

'Change your name then,' suggested Poppy. 'You could have a lovely red cross embroidered on your tunic and be the Red Cross Knight instead.'

The knight wiped his fingers daintily on a paper napkin. He looked thoughtful.

'Thank you for the excellent lunch

and the advice. I think I'll do as you suggest. Only I'll need a new suit of armour. This one's hardly shining any more.' He looked with distaste at the rusting heap of metal he had climbed out of.

'It's a lovely day,' said Poppy, helpfully, 'why not get rid of it now?'

The knight suddenly picked up all the armour, the sword, the shield, the lance and the metal thing with knobs on and hurled them into the moat.

'There,' he said, panting. 'Now I'm off to get a nice loose tunic and a squire.'

He leapt onto his horse in his long-johns and with a gracious wave to Poppy, rode off to become the other sort of knight.

Chapter Four

POPPY WAS PLEASED with the way
the knight adventure had worked out.
But the very next day the king
summoned Poppy to another interview
with him and the Queen. They both
looked very serious.

'My dear,' said the King.
'Something has . . . er . . . turned
up.'

'A dragon,' said the Queen.

Poppy felt a delicious thrill run up
and down her backbone.

'It is roaring around the kingdom,
breathing fire, and destroying houses
and crops,' said the Queen.

'There is only one traditional way of

getting rid of a dragon,' said the King.

'Advertising,' said the Queen. 'We shall advertise for a prince to come and kill it. And as princes can't be expected to give their services for nothing, there has to be a reward.'

'Reward?' said Poppy.

'The reward,' said the Queen, 'is you.'

'I refuse to be a reward,' said Poppy stamping her foot. 'Anyway why can't I get rid of the dragon? I got rid of the ogre and the knight.'

'This is quite different, my dear,' said the King, 'much more dangerous.'

'Besides,' said the Queen, 'it is not ladylike to kill dragons.'

'Who said anything about killing it?' muttered Poppy, who liked animals.

But it was no good. This time she

couldn't persuade her parents to
change their minds. The beautiful
dresses were got out again and Poppy
met an awful lot of princes. It was
very boring and she was usually
horrid to them. If they were young,
she put her tongue out and crossed her
eyes at them while the King and
Queen weren't looking. If they were
old, she made them play hide-and-seek
and hunt the thimble until they were

tired out. No one made any attempt to kill the dragon. They seemed to go off the idea of the reward when they met the princess. One day, Poppy was playing outdoors in her old clothes for a treat, when she heard the familiar sound of a herald announcing another prince. When her mother came to find her she refused to change her clothes, but she had to go indoors and meet the prince.

Prince Robin was about the same age as Poppy. When they were introduced, Princess Poppy stuck out her tongue and crossed her eyes. Prince Robin waggled his ears and pulled his mouth out with his fingers.

'Would you like to play outdoors?' said Poppy.

'Yes, please,' said Robin.

When they were tired of hide-and-

seek and tree-climbing Poppy said,
'Are you going ahead with this dragon
business?'

'No option,' said Robin. 'My father
says it's traditional. Part of my
princely duties, or something.'

'Mm,' said Poppy, 'my father's the
same. I don't see why they are all so
keen on killing the dragon, though. I'd
love to see him.'

'Yes, I don't want to kill him,' said
Robin. 'I'm against blood-sports.'

'Why don't I come with you
tomorrow then?' said Poppy. 'Perhaps
we could persuade him to go away
without hurting him?'

Chapter Five

SO THE NEXT morning Robin set out on his white horse while Poppy waved to him from the battlements. As soon as he was out of sight, Poppy shut herself in her room, changed her clothes and escaped down a ladder of knotted sheets.

Together they reached the place where the dragon had last been seen. There was a terrible mess of burnt trees and trampled houses. Robin got out some food from his saddle bags and the prince and princess settled down for a nice lunch of cheese and tomato rolls and lemonade. They were just brushing away the crumbs when they heard a terrible crashing noise.

Coming through what was left of the trees was a dragon. They had never seen one before but, there is no mistaking one when you meet it.

'Hello,' said Poppy. 'Do you mind standing a bit further away? You're boiling the lemonade.'

'Sorry,' said the dragon. 'I can't help it.'

'Must be very awkward breathing fire every time you open your mouth,' said Prince Robin, sympathetically.

'It's a terrible nuisance,' roared the dragon, and Poppy and the prince had to jump back out of the way of the flames.

'I say, mind the horse,' said Robin,
'you don't want to roast him, do you?'

'Sorry,' whispered the dragon, and
only a tiny puff of smoke came out.

'Hold it right there,' said Poppy.
'I've got an idea.'

She walked boldly up to the dragon
and looked him in the eye. 'Now don't
say anything. Just nod or shake your
head. Can you write?'

The dragon nodded. Poppy took out a notebook and a rather chewed pencil and gave it to the dragon.

'Now,' said Poppy, 'write down the answers to my questions. Do you want to destroy this kingdom?'

The dragon wrote 'No' in big letters on the first page of Poppy's notebook.

'Good,' said Poppy, 'I thought not.'

'Then why do you do it?' said Robin.

The dragon started to scribble furiously. And this is what he wrote:

'You are the first sensible people I have met in this country. I have a terrible sore throat and a bad cough. Every time I open my mouth to tell someone, they run away screaming. And somehow a lot of things end up getting burnt.'

Poppy and Robin read the page eagerly.

'You know what,' said Poppy, to the dragon, 'you ought to give up smoking.'

The dragon opened his mouth to protest and the prince and princess hastily backed away. The dragon closed his mouth and wrote:

Poppy thought for a bit and then she told Robin her plan.

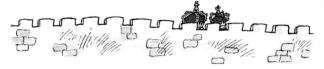

Chapter Six

LATE THAT AFTERNOON, long after
tea-time, the King and Queen were
looking anxiously from the
battlements. Imagine their amazement
when they saw not just Prince Robin
and not just their own daughter, who
should have been in her bedroom, but
also a very meek dragon returning to
the castle.

'Your Majesties,' called Robin, 'have
no fear! This dragon is quite safe. He
is a reformed character.'

The Queen was very pleased. 'Well
done, Prince Robin!' she cried. 'You
have tamed the dragon which is just as
good as killing it.'

'Better, really,' said the dragon,

under his breath, which was no longer fiery.

'You have won our daughter's hand in marriage,' said the King.

'Rubbish,' said Poppy, briskly. 'He has done no such thing.'

'Really!' said the Queen.

'Tradition demands it,' said the King.

'Poppy's right,' said Robin. 'She's the one who solved the problem of the dragon. She took him underwater-bathing in the lake. It worked marvellously. He's quite put out now.'

The Queen was put out too. 'Well, what was the point of bringing him here?' she said.

'Just to show you,' said Poppy. 'This extremely polite dragon has agreed, in return for my curing his cough and sore throat, to remain in our kingdom and provide central heating for the people in winter. If you would be so kind, father, as to call up the royal engineer, we could get down to designing the necessary pipe system. The summer's nearly over. No time to lose.'

The King and the Queen gaped at one another. This dragon business wasn't working out as usual at all.

'So you don't want Poppy's hand as a reward?' the King asked Robin.

'Why doesn't anyone listen to *me*,' said Poppy, crossly.

'Your Majesty, I haven't earned a reward,' said Robin firmly. 'It was all your daughter's doing. Besides, I'm too young to get married. But I don't know what my father will say if I return home empty-handed.'

The dragon gave Robin a scaly nudge. 'I think I might be able to help,' he said. 'Traditionally dragons sit on large heaps of gold. You know, sleep for hundreds of years, that sort of thing. Well, I couldn't sleep for that dreadful cough of mine. So I got up off my gold and came looking for help. But it's not far away and you

can certainly have some of it to take home.'

'Would you mind, Poppy?' asked Robin. 'After all, it was you who cured him.'

'It's reward enough for me not to be married off to any old prince who comes along,' said Poppy. 'No offence to you, Robin, of course.'

'None taken,' said Robin. 'I'll take the gold instead. But I hope I can come and see you again. I don't know when I've enjoyed an adventure more.'

'Same here,' said Poppy and they shook hands on it.

Robin went off with the dragon to collect his treasure.

'Right, that's that,' said Poppy. 'What's for tea? I'm starving.'